One boy, called Kaito, did more than just dream.
"I'm pretty **tough**," he said to himself.
"I'll try my luck at the wrestling tournament in Kyoto."

And this skinny boy left
his village and set out for
the great city of Kyoto.

After a while Kaito came to a steep hill, where he saw a girl balancing a bucket of water on her head. She had just filled it from the river.

"Good! I'll have someone to talk to," he thought. "She looks friendly."

Jessica Souhami studied at the Central School of Art and Design, and went on to set up a touring shadow puppet company, featuring music and a storyteller. She is internationally acclaimed for her folk-tale retellings, bringing some of the world's greatest stories to a young audience. Her many books for Frances Lincoln include *Foxy!*, *Sausages*, *The Sticky Doll Trap*, *The Little Little House*, *Old MacDonald*, *No Dinner!*, *The Leopard's Drum* – the classic West-African tale which has just celebrated its twentieth anniversary – and *Rama and the Demon King*. Jessica lives in north London.

JESSICA SOUHAMI

Frances Lincoln
Children's Books

Long ago in Japan, many boys dreamed of becoming Champion Wrestlers. You see, Champion Wrestlers were celebrities. They became very rich and very, very famous – even more famous than pop stars and film stars are today.

Then a silly idea came into Kaito's head.
"That bucket's full. She has to balance it very carefully.
I could tickle her... she'd have to laugh...
and I'd laugh... and she'd try not to wobble...
It would be so funny!" Then he frowned. "No... I mustn't...
she might spill the water and get cross."

But Kaito couldn't resist the temptation.
He crept nearer to the girl and stretched out his hand...

AND...

Wham!

The girl slammed her arm down firmly,
trapping Kaito's hand. Much to his amazement
Kaito could not pull his hand free.
The girl did not spill a single drop of water.

She just walked on up the hill,
dragging poor Kaito behind her.

"HEY!" yelled Kaito,
"Who are you? Let me go!"

The girl giggled.
"I'm Hana," she said. "Who are you?"
"I'm Kaito. I'm going to Kyoto for the wrestling tournament."
"Are you sure?" she asked. "Wrestling is very dangerous, you know. There'll be huge, strong wrestlers in Kyoto. And I don't want to be rude, but you do look a little feeble."

Kaito was speechless.

And so Hana dragged Kaito all the way to her cottage at the very top of the hill.

Inside, Hana looked Kaito up and down.
"Hmmm!" she said. "I *might* be able to help you.
There are three weeks until the tournament,
and *maybe* I can toughen you up. No promises though.
I can't work miracles and you really are very weedy."

"Oh dear," sighed Kaito.
"Well, I've nothing to lose."
So he agreed to Hana's plan.
And the next day his training began.

Hana made Kaito run and jump,
kick and stamp, lift and punch.

She fed him on big bowls of fish stew and rice.
At the end of the first week Kaito asked, "Well?"
Hana shook her head. "A long way to go, Kaito."

In the second week Hana fed him on enormous bowls of tough meat and half-cooked rice.
At the end of the week Kaito asked, "Well?"
But Hana shook her head. "Not yet, Kaito."

In the third week Hana fed him on **gigantic** bowls of raw rice and the boniest fish and meat stews.
And Kaito asked, "Well?"
Hana said…

"**YES!** I think you're ready, Kaito. Good luck for the tournament."

So Kaito set out for Kyoto once more.

In Kyoto all the famous wrestlers were gathered.
They paraded through the streets,
boasting of their strength and showing off
their huge bulk.

They laughed at Kaito.

"Go home, little boy," they sneered,
"before we squash you flat."

Kaito trembled but he stood firm.

The tournament started the very next day.
The rules were simple.
Two wrestlers met in the ring.
Each tried to push the other
out of the ring or onto the floor.
The winner stayed in to fight
the next man.

The last wrestler left standing
would be the new champion.

The first wrestler was so **huge** and scary
that Kaito looked tiny beside him.

BUT, when Kaito gave him a little push,
this enormous man

flew out of the ring

as if a giant had attacked him!

KAITO HAD WON!

Kaito beat all the other wrestlers. . .

Well, all but two who said that unfortunately they couldn't stay to wrestle this year as they suddenly had very urgent and important things to do at home.

KAITO WAS CHAMPION!

An important man came from the palace with Kaito's prize.

"The Emperor says that he has never seen such great wrestling," he said. "He invites you to come and live at the court as his Imperial Champion."

"I'm deeply honoured," replied Kaito, "but I miss my village and the countryside. I must take this prize to Hana, who truly deserves it, and then I'll go home."

So Kaito set out for Hana's cottage,
holding tight to the casket.

As he came near he saw her
running to meet him...

"WELCOME BACK, CHAMPION!" she called.

"WELCOME BACK, THE STRONGEST **BOY** IN THE WORLD!"

Kaito laughed and thanked Hana
for making his dream come true.

And, while Hana stayed in the hills
busily clearing huge rocks from her fields
Kaito continued his journey home.

But did Kaito become rich and famous?

Well, the country gods love good wrestling
and they blessed Kaito's village.
The crops grew tall, the people were happy –
and the story of Champion Kaito
became famous.

And now you know it too!

ABOUT *THE STRONGEST BOY IN THE WORLD*

This story is based on a famous Japanese tale first recorded in the 13th century. There are some famous drawings and prints of this tale – for example by Hokusai and Tsukioka Yoshitoshi.

The original story is about a grown-up warrior, who is on his way to a wrestling tournament when he meets a beautiful widow, one of the legendary strong women of Japanese myth. She teaches him how to be invincible.

For centuries Japanese Sumo wrestlers have been regarded as celebrities. So, just as modern boys in the west may dream of becoming pop stars or footballers I thought it would be fun to make the hero a boy who seeks celebrity as a wrestler. My hero is a rather puny boy called Kaito and the heroine a young woman called Hana – who is just as tough as the original heroine of the tale.

Sumo wrestling bouts really can be as brief as described.

And it is said that the gods bless successful wrestlers and make their villages prosper.

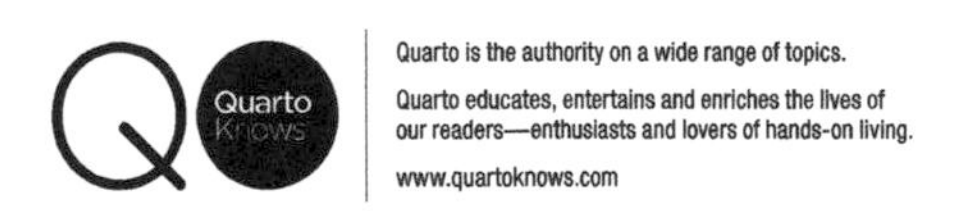

JANETTA OTTER-BARRY BOOKS

First published in Great Britain and in the USA in 2014 by
Frances Lincoln Children's Books, 74-77 White Lion Street, London N1 9PF
www.franceslincoln.com

This paperback edition first published in Great Britain and in the USA in 2015

A catalogue record for this book is available from the British Library.

ISBN 978-1-84780-603-1

Illustrated with collage of Ingres papers hand-painted with watercolour inks and graphite pencil

Set in Bell Gothic

Printed and bound by CPI Group (UK) Ltd, Croydon, CR0 4YY

MORE BEAUTIFUL PICTURE BOOKS BY JESSICA SOUHAMI PUBLISHED BY FRANCES LINCOLN CHILDREN'S BOOKS

Foxy!
978-1-84780-498-3

"An excellent spin on a familiar trickster story"
– *Kirkus Starred Review*

"Bright colours in tropical hues, and a multicultural cast of characters, give this folk tale a smart, modern look and feel" – *Booklist*

"Fresh and exciting" – *English 4-11*

The Sticky Doll Trap
978-1-84780-017-6

"The Matisse-bright pictures and Jessica Souhami's faultless ear for storytelling will give pleasure to children of three and up." – *The Times*

" A spellbinder to stick with!" – *INIS*